This Little Tiger book belongs to:

_____

_____

_____

To Lucy and Jonny ~ A R

For my parents Erich and Heide Haas ~ C H

LITTLE TIGER PRESS
1 The Coda Centre, 189 Munster Road, London SW6 6AW
www.littletiger.co.uk

First published in Great Britain 2008
This edition published 2014
by Little Tiger Press, London

Printed in China • LTP/1900/0832/0114

10 9 8 7 6 5 4 3 2 1

IT'S TIME TO SLEEP, YOU CRAZY SHEEP!

Alison Ritchie   Cornelia Haas

LITTLE TIGER PRESS

Tucked in bed, all warm and snug,
Phoebe tries to sleep.
She shuts her eyes, but she's not tired:
she needs to count her sheep!

But Phoebe's sheep have other plans.
They're bored of jumping gates.
They're heading for the ice rink,
and putting on their skates.

They slip and slide, they zip and glide,
their feet a tangled blur.
They skim along the frozen ice,
like fluffy balls of fur.

Now they're revving up their bikes.
They like to travel fast!

"Wait!" cries Phoebe, but her sheep just wave as they whizz past.

They've reached the highest cliff top now.
"Come **back** here!" Phoebe cries.
But off they float, like clouds on legs,
to drift across the skies.

Next it's time for ballet,
and those silly, woolly ewes
Spring and prance, whirl and dance
in dainty ballet shoes.

"Stop it, stop it!" Phoebe wails.
"Let me count you, please!"
But her sheep zoom down the slope,
zig-zagging through the trees.

BOING!

Bouncing on a trampoline,
up and down they go.
Like daring circus acrobats,
they're putting on a show!

Off they go to match day,
to dribble, duck, and dive.
Another goal! The whistle blows:
the home team wins six-five.

"Stop!" shouts Phoebe. "Stop it now!
I'm still wide awake!"
But Phoebe's sheep are boiling hot,
and flocking to the lake.

With double flips and somersaults,
into the lake they leap.
One by one, splish splash splosh,
Phoebe counts her sheep!

At last poor Phoebe's quiet.
She doesn't make a peep.
Her eyes are closed, she's nodded off.
Phoebe is asleep!

"Hooray!" cheer Phoebe's naughty sheep.
Their night has just begun.
"Let's all be on our way," they say.
"It's time to have some FUN!"